Willa
and Old Miss Annie

Willa
and Old Miss Annie

Berlie Doherty

Illustrated by Kim Lewis

Catnip

CATNIP BOOKS
Published by Catnip Publishing Ltd.
320 City Road
London
EC1V 2NZ

First published 1994 by Walker Books Ltd
This edition published 2011

5 7 9 8 6 4

Text copyright © 1994 Berlie Doherty
Illustrations copyright © 1994 Kim Lewis
Cover illustration copyright © 2011 Kim Lewis

A CIP catalogue record of this book is available from the British Library.

ISBN 978-1-84647-119-3

Printed and bound by CPI Group (UK) Ltd, Croydon, CR0 4YY

www.catnippublishing.co.uk

For Willa, for Amy and for the
Millhouse Animal Sanctuary in Sheffield

Contents

Joshua

This is the story of a little girl called Willa, who has a friend called Old Miss Annie. She has another friend called Joshua. But it wasn't always like this. When Willa first met Old Miss Annie she was afraid of her. And when she first met Joshua she thought he was a ghost.

Willa was afraid of Old Miss Annie because her hair was like wool and because her voice was full of tiny words. The words were so tiny that they were hardly there at all. They were like secrets. And her hands were full of bumps. Have you ever seen a twig that is all bent and twisted and full of bumps? If you have, then you will know what Old Miss Annie's hands were like. That was why Willa was afraid of her.

And Willa thought Joshua was a ghost because she saw him in Miss Annie's garden in the dark. The sky was full of stars and the moon looked like a boat that night. There was something white in Miss Annie's garden and it seemed to be dancing. That was why Willa thought that Joshua was a ghost. And in the night Joshua cried, and Willa thought it was a ghost crying.

So this is the story of how Willa met Old Miss Annie and became her friend. But first she had to say goodbye to Rose.

Willa says goodbye to Rose

Mum and Dad had bought a house in a big town, far away. They would have to drive all day to get to the new house, and when they got there they would be in another country. They would cross over many rivers and drive along many roads. The sky would turn black and all the stars would come out, before they reached the house in the town where Willa was going to live.

But first she had to say goodbye to Rose. Rose came upstairs to her room with her. They packed all Willa's toys in a big trunk.

'It looks like a box of treasures,' said Rose.

'It is,' said Willa.

She put a Bear called Billy on the top of all the toys and closed the lid of the trunk. The removal men carried it downstairs to the van that would take it to Willa's new house.

There was no bed in the room because that was already in the removal van, so Rose and Willa sat on the floor and held hands. They cried because they would never see each other again.

When they went downstairs they felt shy of each other. Willa followed Mum and Dad to the car and she didn't know what to say to Rose. It was as if they had never been friends at all. But when they were driving to the new house, over all the rivers and through all the strange cities, Willa kept thinking about Rose. The sky turned black and all the stars came out. They reached another country.

Willa knew then that she would never have another friend like Rose again. And it was true.

By the time they arrived at the new house Willa was fast asleep. Mum carried her up to her new bedroom and put her in her own

bed. Dad carried up the trunk. He opened
it and looked at all the toys that were like
treasures. Then he picked out a Bear called
Billy and put him on Willa's pillow.

When Willa woke up she didn't know
where she was. The ceiling was too high.
The window was too far away. The walls
had flowers on instead of clowns. Then
she found a Bear called Billy on her pillow
and she hugged him. She remembered that
she would never see Rose again and she
began to cry. Outside in a garden she heard
something else crying. It sounded like a little,
lost, ghosty child.

Willa looks for a friend

Mum and Dad and Willa were busy all day,
unpacking boxes and sorting things out.

'We'll paint all the doors and paper all

the walls,' said Dad. 'And you can choose the colours for your room, Willa.'

'It'll soon look like home,' Mum told her.

But Willa knew it would never look like home. That afternoon she went with Mum to the shops at the top of the road.

'We'll see if we can find some friends for you,' Mum said.

But they looked in every front garden that they passed, and there was no sign anywhere of any children for Willa to play with.

'Don't worry,' Mum said. 'You'll soon make friends when you start at the school.'

'I don't want a friend,' said Willa.

She only wanted one friend, and that was Rose, who lived in another country far away over all the rivers.

That night Willa hugged a Bear called Billy, and listened to the sound of sad, ghosty crying in somebody's garden.

Old Miss Annie

Next day Willa met Old Miss Annie for the very first time. She heard a knock at the door, and saw Mum bringing an old lady into the kitchen. She was afraid of her. The lady had hair like wool. Willa had never seen hair like that before. And when the old lady spoke, her voice was full of tiny words. They were so tiny that you could hardly hear them. They were more like secrets. Willa put her hands over her ears so she couldn't hear the tiny voice.

Old Miss Annie sat down on the new kitchen chair and peered at Willa as if she couldn't quite see her.

'Would you like a cup of tea, Miss Annie?' Mum said.

'I would,' said Miss Annie, in her tiny voice.

That was when Willa saw Miss Annie's

hands. They were full of bumps, like a twig that's all bent and twisted. Willa closed her eyes so she couldn't see them. And that was when Miss Annie told Willa one of her secrets. The words were so tiny that Willa could hardly hear them, but what she thought Miss Annie said was: 'Do you know what I've got in my garden? A ghost!'

The ghost in the garden

That night when Willa was in bed she heard the sound of crying in someone's garden. It was such a sad, lost, lonely cry. She and a Bear called Billy climbed out of bed to have a look through the window. The sky was full of stars, and the moon was like a boat that night. And in one of the gardens she saw a white shape. Willa clutched a Bear called Billy.

'It's the ghost!' she whispered.

Then the white shape began to move, just as if it were dancing.

'Look at the ghost dancing!' whispered Willa.

And then it began to cry, such a sad, lonely, ghosty cry.

'It's the ghost crying,' said Willa. 'Poor ghost!'

Every night Willa looked out of her window and saw the white shape dancing, and every night she heard its sad, lost, lonely, ghosty cry.

One day, when she was going to the shops with Mum, they saw Old Miss Annie coming out of her front door. She came slowly down towards them, peering at them as though she couldn't quite see them. When she remembered who they were, she smiled. Willa held Mum's hand tightly.

'How do you like your new house?' Old

Miss Annie asked Mum. Her voice was so tiny that it was hardly there at all.

'It's lovely,' Mum said. 'But I wish we could find a friend for Willa.'

Willa thought about Rose, who lived far away in another country. She knew she would never see Rose again. She closed her eyes and tried to pretend that it didn't matter. Then Old Miss Annie bent towards her and told her another of her secrets.

'I want you to come and see Joshua,' she whispered.

Willa opened her eyes. She held Mum's hand tighter than ever because she was so afraid of Old Miss Annie, but she asked the question that she wanted to ask.

'Does Joshua live in your garden?' she asked.

Old Miss Annie nodded.

Willa still held Mum's hand tightly.

'I've seen him dancing,' she said.

Old Miss Annie nodded again. Willa saw how pale and smiling her eyes were.

'I've heard him crying in the night,' Willa said.

And then she saw how Old Miss Annie's eyes turned sad.

'I think he's lonely,' Old Miss Annie said, and the words were so tiny that they were more like secrets that had never been told to anyone else before.

Old Miss Annie held out her hand. It was full of bumps, just like a twig that's all twisted. Even though Willa was afraid of Old Miss Annie she liked the way her eyes looked sad and smiling at the same time.

'You go and see Joshua,' said Mum. 'And I'll call for you when I come back from the shops.'

So Willa let go of Mum's hand and

followed Old Miss Annie up her path and round to the garden at the back. And that was how she met Joshua.

Joshua the ghost

Joshua had yellow eyes and a beard like white silk. He had horns that twisted round themselves, and a big mouth like a saucer. He was tied by a rope to a post under the trees in Miss Annie's little garden, and when he tried to move away from it he jumped in the air. It was just as if he were dancing. And then he gave his sad cry, and Willa felt as if she were crying too.

'Poor ghost,' she said.

Old Miss Annie went over to Joshua and patted him, and slipped the rope off the stick. 'I'll move the tether-pin,' she said. 'Then he can have some fresh grass.'

'Why is he tied up?' asked Willa.

'Because he'd eat everything in my garden,' Old Miss Annie chuckled. 'And he'd have hiccups.'

Joshua cried again, and Willa put her hands over her ears.

'Why does he cry so much?' she shouted.

'I think he's lonely,' Old Miss Annie said. 'And this garden is too small for him.'

Willa thought that Joshua didn't look like a ghost at all. He looked like a small white horse, or a big white dog, or a sheep. 'He doesn't look like a ghost,' she said.

Old Miss Annie put her head a little to one side as if she couldn't hear Willa properly. 'We could take him for a walk, if you like,' she said.

They both had to hold onto Joshua's rope. He skipped in front of them, tucking his head down and kicking his legs out.

Willa and Old Miss Annie hung onto his rope and laughed all the way up the road. His feet made little scratching noises on the pavement. Everyone they passed smiled at them and said, 'Hello, Miss Annie,' and 'Hello, Joshua,' and when Old Miss Annie introduced them to Willa they said, 'Hello, Willa,' too, and smiled. Some of them were children.

Willa felt proud to be the one taking Joshua for a walk.

When they got back to Old Miss Annie's house they were both out of breath with running behind Joshua. They put him back in the garden, and that was when Miss Annie told Willa the story of how Joshua came to stay with her.

'One day,' Old Miss Annie said, 'I saw a picture of Joshua in the paper. I fell in love with him! And under the picture it said:

> ## HOME WANTED FOR JOSHUA
> If no home is found for him, he must die.

'I was so sorry for him that I phoned up and Joshua came to stay. I do love him!' Her eyes sparkled. 'But he's lonely, isn't he, Willa?'

Willa nodded.

'He cries all night,' said Old Miss Annie.

Willa nodded again. 'He needs a friend,' she said.

Joshua's new friend

That night Willa told Dad about Joshua. 'He needs to be in a field full of ghosts,' she said.

'I'll see if I can find one,' Dad smiled.

And he did. He put Joshua in the back of his van, and Old Miss Annie and Willa stroked him all the way to the countryside.

They drove past a dark wood and over a bridge and came at last to the farm that belonged to Dad's friend Alison. The farm had a field with three horses in it and another field with goats.

Alison opened the gate to the field that was full of goats and Joshua danced into it, and all the other goats danced down to Joshua like friends.

'You'll come and see him soon, won't you?' Alison said as she waved goodbye to them.

'Joshua's a goat really, isn't he?' said Willa.

Old Miss Annie looked at her and nodded. She put out her hand, that was full of bumps like an old bent twig, and Willa held it tight.

The Bony

There's a little farm in High Lightly, just over the bridge from Johnny Gate. In the farm there's a field full of horses, and another field full of goats. One of the horses is so small that he can run right under the legs of the tallest horse, Humphrey. But he'd rather play with the goats any day, especially with the one called Joshua.

He's as round as a barrel and as brown as a conker. He loves to run so his mane streams like wild grass, and most of all he loves to roll in the mud and kick his legs in the air.

He's very happy now. But it wasn't always so. Once upon a time he didn't even have a name.

This is the story of a Shetland pony, and how he got his name.

Sly Old Silas

The Shetland pony didn't always live in a field full of horses and next to a field full of goats. He once belonged to a man called Silas who lived a wandering sort of life. Silas didn't like houses, and he didn't like people. He lived in a rusty van that smelt of oil. He bought and sold things; that was his job. He bought anything that was going cheap, and he sold it for more. He cheated people a bit, and they didn't like him for it. He was known in the villages that he travelled to as 'Sly Old Silas', but even so, people bought things from him because he had such interesting things to sell. Often they were the sort of things that people dreamed of having, such as clocks with blue faces, or flowers made of real silk, or bells that tinkled in the wind.

When the villagers saw the things that Silas had to sell they usually felt that they couldn't manage another day without them; not because they needed them but because they dreamed about them.

'Golden bells and bouncing balls,' Silas would sing in his froggy voice.

'Chiming clocks and lacy shawls . . .'

And one day he sold something that couldn't be paid for, and that was how he came to get the little Shetland pony.

Silly Molly Pickleby

It all began on the day that Silas came to Johnny Gate and knocked on Molly Pickleby's door. Molly Pickleby was very silly sometimes. She bought things that she couldn't afford, that was her trouble. She found it very hard to resist the things that Silas had to sell. However hard she tried to say no, there was always something that she couldn't manage without, and Silas knew this very well. She heard his froggy song coming along the lane: 'Golden bells and bouncing balls,' and she peered longingly through the window, knowing how his rusty van would be bulging with all kinds of exciting things.

'It's Sly Old Silas,' she said to herself. 'Well, I won't buy anything from him today, thank you! Besides, I haven't any money.'

'Chiming clocks and lacy shawls,' Silas sang in his awful croaky bullfroggy voice.

'No, thanks!' Molly shouted out, standing behind her door. 'Besides, no money.'

'Buckets and pumpkins and teddy bears . . .'

'I won't buy from you, Old Silas,' said Molly, with her back to the door and her hands over her ears. 'Your buckets will be full of holes and your pumpkins will be full of maggots and your teddy bears will have their ears dropping off. Your balls won't bounce and your bells won't ring. I know you. Your clocks will stop and your shawls will let the wind through. I won't buy from you!'

'Candles and kites and rocking chairs . . .'

'Rocking chairs!' Silly Molly Pickleby opened her door and looked. And there, on the top of the pile, was the rocking chair of her dreams.

The rocking chair

Molly Pickleby loved the rocking chair. She imagined sitting by the fire in it in the winter, and sitting in the porch in it in the summer. She imagined herself rocking and creaking in it and singing into the night. How her knitting would grow when she rocked and creaked and sang in that chair! She couldn't do without it.

'I'll have it,' she told Silas. 'How much do you want for it?'

Now Sly Old Silas had found the chair on a dump and all he'd had to do was to polish it up and mend one of the rockers, but even so he told Molly a price that was far too high.

'It's a nice little chair,' he coaxed her. 'It's worth every penny.'

Molly Pickleby knew that she didn't have

enough money to buy the chair, not even if she sold her pig, which she loved too much to take to market anyway. And just when she was feeling sad and gloomy she remembered that she had something in the yard that she didn't want at all, that had belonged to her son before he went away to China. She felt as sly as Silas then, knowing that she could trick him as much as he always tried to trick her.

'I have no money for you, Silas,' she said, sitting in the rocking chair and picking up her knitting, because she knew now that the chair was hers. 'But I have something in my yard that you could really do with.'

'What's that?' asked Silas, warming his red hands in front of Molly's fire, and watching her knitting grow.

'A horse, Silas. I have a horse for you.'

'A horse!' Silas had to turn away to hide

the gleam in his eyes. *Silly Molly Pickleby!* he thought to himself. *A horse is worth ten times as much as the best rocking chair in the world, and this one is just a scrap from a dump, with a patched-up rocker!*

'Is it an old horse?'

'Oh, no,' said Molly. She tied some red wool to the scarf she was knitting, making a lovely warm pattern. 'It's two years old.'

Silas rubbed his chin till all the black bristles scraped and sparked. 'Ah, then. It must be lame.'

Molly creaked a little, and sang a tune to herself. 'He skips along like a newborn lamb,' she said.

'Then it has a bad temper?'

'He's as sweet as springtime, I tell you.'

Silas turned round to warm his backside by the fire. He saw himself on the horse of his dreams, riding from village to village and chanting out his wares. He would sell his rusty old van and buy a bright wooden caravan instead, and he would let the horse of his dreams pull it along for him.

'Where is he then?' Sly Silas peered out of the back window into Molly Pickleby's yard, and knew that there was no room there for the horse of his dreams.

'At this very moment my son is riding him over the moors,' Molly said. Then, because that was such a lie, she decided to risk telling Silas a little bit of the truth. 'He's a lovely little horse,' she added.

'Little, did you say?'

'What would you want with a great big carthorse, eh? You're a little man yourself, Silas.'

So he is, she thought. *Little and mean and sly.* She poked him playfully with one of her needles and laughed up at him.

'I'll have him!' said Silas. 'Bring him to my van tonight.'

The little dwarfy horse

Molly Pickleby rocked and sang and knitted till there was no more light to see by. Then she put down her knitting and went into the yard and opened the door of her shed. There was the Shetland pony, blinking in the light she held up to him. He trotted up to her, nuzzling in her skirt pockets, which were just the right height for him, hoping to find carrots there.

'Come on,' she said. 'I've found another home for you. You're no use to me, little dwarfy horse that you are.'

She led the pony over the field where Sly Old Silas had parked his van. He had lifted the bed out from under the pile of things he had to sell and was fast asleep on it, curled up under a heap of rugs and rags and second-hand clothes, right in the middle of the field. She crept up and tied the pony's rope to the bedpost.

'Is that you, Molly Pickleby?' Silas muttered in his sleep.

'It is. It is.'

'And have you brought me my horse?'

'I have. I have. I have. Can't you hear him munching just by your ear?'

Silas could. He could hear horsy munchy jaws by his ear and he could feel horsy tickly breath on his cheek and he was satisfied.

Molly chuckled to herself and crept away.

The next day she was woken up by such a sound of thumping and banging on her door that if she hadn't been expecting it she would have died of fright.

'Who is it?' she asked, not stirring from her bed.

'That's not a horse, Molly Pickleby, and well you know it.'

Molly wriggled her toes about in her warm sheets. 'It is. It is. It's every inch a horse.'

'It's a midget! It's no bigger than a pig!' Silas roared. 'It's no good to me! I want my chair back.'

Molly rolled over in her bed, punching her pillow to make it a bit more comfortable. 'You struck a bargain with me, Silas,' she reminded him. 'And you must stand by it. I swapped a horse for a chair, and fair is fair. If you go back on your word there's not a woman in this village who will buy from you again, not one. Nor in any of the villages around, I'll make quite sure of that.'

Silas knew she was right. He kicked her door one last time and stomped off to the field, where the Shetland pony was rolling about in the mud with its legs in the air.

'Call that a horse!' Silas groaned. 'I'll be a laughing stock.'

He hitched the pony to his van and drove slowly along, and the pony ambled along behind, as if it had all the time in the world to get from Johnny Gate to High Lightly, never mind across the moors to Bakewell.

'Clocks and scarfs and rings and shells,' Silas sang, without much cheer in his croaky old voice.

The pony stopped to eat some grass and Silas had to screech his van to a halt. He wound down his window.

'Walk, you goblin!' he shouted. 'Get a move on, you hairy gnome!'

The little pony tried to nibble Silas's chin.

'Sweet as springtime!' Silas moaned. 'Frisky as a lamb! You're too midgety for me to ride you. You're too dwarfy to pull a cart.

You're as slow as a slug. I'll be a laughing stock for miles around.'

After an hour of hardly getting anywhere at all, Silas had had enough. He untied the pony and led him into the woods. There he tied his rope to the stump of a tree.

'I can't be doing with you,' he grumbled. 'You can just stay there till I get back – if I ever come this way again.' And off he went, whistling a little bit because he was pleased that he wouldn't be a laughing stock after all. The Shetland pony munched the grass around the tree stump.

'Beds and birds and bells and balls . . .' the pony could hear, fainter and fainter.

That night, when Molly Pickleby sat in her rocking chair with her knitting in her hand, she heard a great crack! The next minute she was sprawling on the floor, and there was the rocking chair, in pieces all around her.

In the dark woods an owl began to hoot. The badger sniffed out of its sett and the fox crept from its lair. The pony that was as brown as a conker lifted a hoof so he could rest on its tip. He bowed his head so his long dark hair fell forward like a curtain over his eyes. And soon he slept.

The dark woods

The pony still didn't have a name. This is how he got one. It has something to do with a big boy called Hodkin, and with a little girl called Willa and an old lady with hair like wool. This is what happened.

The days grew shorter and greyer, and the nights grew longer and colder. Winter came. The little Shetland pony tied to the tree stump in the middle of the dark woods became thin and sad. He'd eaten all the grass that grew round his tree, and although he tugged and tugged at his rope he couldn't reach any new grass. His coat was long and matted. Soon he was so thin that his bones poked through his skin. He looked like a bundle of brown sticks. And where the rope was fastened round his neck, and he'd tried to pull away to reach the grass, he had a red sore. He stood with his head hanging low, too weak to care.

One day it began to snow. Huge snowflakes drifted down like birds from the sky. They filled the trees, they filled the hedges, they piled up on the ground, higher and higher. The Shetland pony began to move, trying to keep warm. He turned himself round and round, and the snow piled up round him like the walls of a castle, and when he was too weak to stand any more his legs that were like brown sticks bundled up underneath him and he fell to the ground.

Big Boy Hodkin

That could have been the end of the story, but that afternoon a big boy called Hodkin came whistling through the woods in search of holly for his mother's kitchen. He saw the stump of the tree with the rope dangling from it and he went to have a look. He scrambled up the wall of snow that looked like a castle and he nearly fell down the other side of it with surprise, because stretched out on the ground below him was the smallest, thinnest horse he'd ever seen. He couldn't even tell whether it was alive or dead.

'Poor little fing!' he said out loud. 'Poor little skinny starving fing!'

He slid down from the wall and ran round in the snow trying to find something he could use to lift up the pony. There was nothing. The slopes of the wall of snow were slippery, and he was frightened of sliding down on top of the pony and hurting him. He didn't know what to do.

Then he had the best idea of his life. He took off his jacket and lowered it down to spread across the pony like a blanket. Then he ran to find help.

It was hard to run through the snow. It came up to his knees and piled inside his boots, and he kept losing his balance and falling. At last he came to the lane and there he had the second best idea of his life. He broke a twig off a tree and wrote a message in the snow. He couldn't write very well but this is what the message said:

Helb the bony

And he drew an arrow pointing into the woods. Then he slithered and slid as fast as he could to get to his home, which was on the other side of the hill.

Help the pony

And that was when the amazing thing happened. Along the lane in the drifting bird-feather snow came an old lady and a little girl. The old lady had hair like wool and it sparkled where the snowflakes clung to it. Her hands were full of bumps, like a twig that's all bent and twisted. She and the little girl walked carefully along the slippery lane that led to Johnny Gate.

They had come from town with the girl's father, but the van had stuck in a snow-pile and was being dug out bit by bit. There was nothing they could do to help, because one was too old and one was too small, and so they had set off together to do what they had come to do, and they clung to each other so that neither of them fell over, and they laughed a lot, and their breath hung in the air like smoke.

'Are you happy, Willa?' asked Old Miss Annie. She looked down at Willa, her eyes sparkling, her cheeks bright with the cold. 'I hope so, because I am!'

'So am I!' said Willa. And then she saw the message. 'What does that say?' she asked.

It was nearly covered up with snow. Old Miss Annie brushed the snow aside as lightly as she could.

'Well, it says "helb the bony",' she said. 'But it can't mean that.'

'What's a bony?' said Willa.

'There's an arrow,' said Miss Annie. 'We could follow it and see.'

Willa and Old Miss Annie clambered into the woods in the direction of the arrow.

Everything was deep and white and silent; the snow lay in mounds beneath the trees like sleeping swans with outstretched wings.

'Isn't it lovely!' said Old Miss Annie, in her tiny, whispery voice, catching her breath because it was so hard for her to walk and because the woods were beautiful that day.

'But where's the bony?' asked Willa.

They saw Hodkin's footsteps scooping out deep hollows and walked along in them, lifting their feet up as high as they could into each step. It was hard work and they both had to stop for breath. The steps led them to the wall of snow that looked like a castle, and to the rope trailing from the tree stump. They knew then that the bony had been found.

Willa scrambled up the wall of snow first. She looked down and bit her lip. Even with Hodkin's coat thrown across it she could see how thin the pony was.

'Here's the bony,' she said as Old Miss Annie climbed up behind her. 'It's a little horse, all skin and bone.'

'Poor little thing,' said Old Miss Annie. Her voice was so sad that it was hardly there at all. 'It's a Shetland pony, Willa, and somebody has left it to starve.'

She took off her scarf and draped it across the pony's neck, and Willa took off her woollen hat and dropped it on its head. Then they slid back down the castle wall and through the tracks made by Hodkin's feet and along the slithery lane, stopping for breath and pulling each other forward, panting and slipping all the way to Dad's van. There it was, half in and half out of a snow drift, and there was Dad, red-faced with digging, and all the time the snow was drifting down like feathers around them.

'Daddy, Daddy!' Willa shouted. 'Come and help the bony!'

'Yes,' said Old Miss Annie, in her whispery voice. 'Help the pony or it will die.'

Seven deeds to save the bony

Old Miss Annie carried a rug that she wore round her knees in the van. Willa pulled the sledge that was in the back. Her father brought his snow shovel. As they trudged back along the lane to the dark woods they met Big Boy Hodkin, who had run and slid and skidded all the way from his home over the hill with a hot-water bottle and a flask of warm, sweet, milky bread and between them they did seven deeds to save the bony's life:

Willa's father dug down the wall of snow that was sheltering the bony like a castle.

He and Big Boy Hodkin lifted the bony onto Willa's sledge.

Old Miss Annie dipped her twiggy fingers

into Big Boy Hodkin's flask of warm, sweet, milky bread and dabbed them on the bony's lips.

Willa tucked Old Miss Annie's rug round him. Big Boy Hodkin slipped his hot-water bottle inside the rug.

Big Boy Hodkin, Willa, her father and Old Miss Annie heaved and pulled at the sledge to get it out of the dark woods where the snow lay like swans with outstretched wings. And they pulled the sledge all the way to the farm in High Lightly, where Alison lived with her fields of goats and horses.

Alison's farm

As soon as they reached the farm gates Willa let go of her part of the sledge rope and ran to find Alison. She was in the stables, forking golden straw into bales for the animals.

'Hello, Willa,' she said. 'I didn't expect to see you on a snowy day like this. I've brought all the animals in, and it doesn't look as if I'll be letting them out again for a long time.'

'Come and look at the bony,' said Willa. She took Alison's hand and tugged her down to the gate where Old Miss Annie and Willa's father and Big Boy Hodkin were struggling to pull the sledge through a soft mound of snow.

Willa squeezed Alison's hand. 'Please, Alison,' she said. 'Make Bony better.'

Alison knelt down and lifted the corner of Old Miss Annie's rug. She saw the little pony, all skin and bones like a bundle of broken sticks. She saw the red mark on his neck from where the rope had rubbed it.

'I think it's too late, Willa,' she said. 'I don't think there's anything I can do.'

'Please try!'

'I can rub tea tree oil into his nasty wound,' said Alison. 'And I can rub oil of lavender into his skin to make it good again. I can find him somewhere dry and warm to sleep. But I don't know if I can make Bony live, Willa, I really don't. I'm sorry.'

'Please!'

'And I haven't much room. He'll have to share a stable.' She helped to pull the sledge across the yard and opened one of the stable doors, and there in the sweet-smelling dark was a pale, ghosty shape. Willa could see his yellow eyes and his beard that was like white silk, and when she ran up to him she could see how his horns twisted round themselves, and that his big mouth looked like a saucer.

'Joshua! It's Joshua!' she said. Willa ran to him and he nuzzled her. 'We've brought a friend for you, Joshua,' Willa whispered. 'Take care of him, won't you?'

Her father and Alison and Big Boy Hodkin lifted up the Shetland pony and laid him on a bed of straw.

Old Miss Annie shouts at Molly

You might think that is the end of the story, but it isn't.

Old Miss Annie was very angry to think that anybody could have left the Shetland pony to die in such a way. 'Who could have done it?' she asked. 'Who could have owned him and been so cruel to him?'

Big Boy Hodkin's eyes were round with importance. 'I think I know!' he said. 'I know someone who was said to have a little horse like this, anyway. She used to keep him in a shed in her garden, or so I'm told.'

'Tell me who it is,' said Old Miss Annie in her tiny voice. 'And I'll go and shout at her.'

'Her name's Molly Pickleby,' said Big Boy Hodkin. 'She's mean and she's silly, but I don't think she'd do a cruel thing like that.'

Alison persuaded Old Miss Annie and Willa to have a hot drink and a little lie down before they set off again, because one was very old and one was very small, and Willa's father and Big Boy Hodkin agreed to have a warm mince pie each while they waited. But it wasn't long before Old Miss Annie was knocking on Molly Pickleby's door, with Willa at her side.

Molly Pickleby was surprised to have visitors on such a cold day, when the ground was thick with snow and the sky was full of feathery white flakes. She put down her knitting and would have offered them both a cup of tea, but Old Miss Annie hadn't come for a chat.

'Have you got a horse?' she asked as soon

as the door was opened. 'A very little horse, just the size of Willa here? A horse that is brown like a conker?'

'No,' said Molly, sensing trouble. 'I've got a pig, but she's pink.'

'A little brown Shetland pony? I'm told you used to have one in your shed.'

'Oh, that one!' Molly Pickleby could tell by the look on Miss Annie's face that she wouldn't get anywhere by telling lies. 'That brown one. Yes. Brown as a conker, you say? Yes. I used to have one. Why?'

'Well, I've just stolen it,' said Miss Annie. 'It was tied to a tree in the woods and it was just about to die.'

'I don't believe it,' gasped Molly, with sudden real tears in her eyes. 'Frisky as a newborn lamb. Sweet as springtime, he was.'

'He's bony now,' said Willa. 'Like a bundle of broken sticks.'

'Well, don't blame me!' Molly was so upset that she would have sat down if she'd had a chair to sit on. 'It's Sly Old Silas who's done that. I gave him that pony in exchange for a rocking chair, and the rocking chair fell to bits as soon as he'd gone. I nearly broke my back. Look!' And she pointed to the pile of sticks by the fireplace that was all that was left of the rocking chair of her dreams. 'If that man ever comes my way again, I'll beat his head open with those sticks.'

'And did Sly Old Silas know it was a Shetland pony you were giving him?' demanded Old Miss Annie. 'Or did he think it was the horse of his dreams, a big, strong shire horse with legs like trees and a mane like flowing silk? Eh? Did he think the horse would be strong enough to pull him and a cart of furniture all round the villages?'

'I don't know,' muttered Molly. She picked up her knitting and tapped away with her needles. 'He could have asked, couldn't he? If he'd said, "Is it a Shetland pony?" I'd have said, "Yes, it is." I would, I would. I'm an honest woman, I am.'

'You're a very silly woman,' Old Miss Annie said. And then she said, 'If you're an honest woman then I suggest you give him proper payment for the chair. A loaf of new-baked bread would be nice,' she suggested. 'A flask of hot tea. And a nice long scarf. Big Boy Hodkin will show you exactly where to put them.'

She took Willa's hand and they went outside again. Willa's father had managed to rescue the van and was waiting in the road by the bridge for them.

'You didn't shout very hard, Miss Annie,' said Willa.

'Didn't I?' Old Miss Annie rubbed her woolly hair till the snow flew off it like sparks. 'I didn't have to, Willa.' Her voice was full of secrets. 'I think she'll get what she deserves.'

Silly Molly and Sly Old Silas

Molly Pickleby was so upset about Bony that she did as she was told without thinking about it. She put all the things in a sack and Big Boy Hodkin took her to the very tree where Sly Old Silas had tied up the Shetland pony. She knew he was due back in High Lightly soon.

And sure enough, that very night he came trudging through Johnny Gate. He was a very footsore and weary man. His van had broken down in the snow, and he'd had to walk miles and miles with a bundle of goods on his back. His bells had lost their jingle with the damp. His ribbons clung to the sack like wet weeds.

If I'd had a little cart with wheels, that pony could have pulled it along for me, he thought, slipping over for the hundredth time. He had snow inside his coat and down his neck, in his ears and up his nose. He was cold and tired and hungry. *And now it's taken me so long to get here it'll be too late. I shouldn't have left him like that.*

He went to the tree where he'd left the Shetland pony all that time ago, knowing that he wouldn't have a hope of finding him there, and couldn't believe his eyes when he saw the sack. He opened it up and ate the bread and drank the tea, feeling a warm glow inside him. He took out the long red scarf and wrapped it round his neck. He recognised it as the one that Molly Pickleby had been knitting. And now he felt so warm and good and smiling that he decided to go round to her house and thank her.

'So you've come!' she said when she opened the door to him. 'And I hope you're going to say you're sorry for selling me a broken chair, before I beat out your brains with it.'

'I'm sorry, Molly,' he whined. 'If you'll let me, I'll mend it, and it will be the chair of your dreams all right. You'll rock yourself to sleep in it, I promise you that.'

He was right, of course. She stood with her knitting and watched him while he hammered and sawed, and when at last she sat in it and rocked and creaked she could hardly keep her eyes open.

'Could I stay and keep warm?' Old Silas croaked in his froggy voice. 'Because I've no van to sleep in now.'

So Molly let him curl up in front of her

fire, and she rocked and sang and sometimes knitted and sometimes slept. And he stayed on the next day, and the next. And even when the snows had gone, she didn't tell him to leave, and he didn't go. They make a good pair, Old Silas and Molly Pickleby, with him being so sly and her being so silly. As far as I know, he's still there now . . .

A name for the bony

When all the snows had slipped away like birds folding up their wings, and the last of the snowdrops and the first of the primroses were pushing through the earth, on a day that was warm and soft, Willa and Old Miss Annie set off to Alison's farm. They could see Joshua in his field, like a white ghost dancing with the other goats. They could see the big horse Humphrey who was as tall as a tree,

and they could see the other horses Bertie and Emerald. But there was no sign of the bony.

Alison came out to the yard to meet them. Joshua's stable door was closed.

Willa didn't dare ask about the bony.

Alison opened the top door of Joshua's stable and lifted Willa up to have a look in. And there was something wonderful there.

'It's the bony!' Willa shouted. 'Miss Annie! Miss Annie! Come and look at him. He's better! Bony's better!'

Alison unbolted the bottom door and out trotted the Shetland pony. His long hair was brown and gleaming like conkers. His mane hung like a fringe round his eyes. His head came exactly up to Willa's.

'Take him into the field, Willa,' said Alison. 'He'd love a trot round.'

'Perhaps Willa could sit on his back,' Old Miss Annie suggested.

'We'll get a saddle and bridle for him,' Alison said. 'And Willa can come and ride him as often as she wants.'

'Can I? Can I really?' Willa couldn't believe what she was hearing.

'Well, someone's got to ride him,' Old Miss Annie smiled, 'and you're the only one who's small enough.'

'Is he mine now, Miss Annie?' Willa asked, but she said it in a whisper in case she'd made a mistake.

And whether Old Miss Annie heard her or not, she whispered back, 'He's a friend for you, Willa. You wanted a friend, didn't you?'

'He's a friend for Joshua too,' laughed Alison. 'Just his size.'

Joshua had come dancing down the field and the bony set off at a round rolling trot to meet him, his mane flopping and lifting as he ran, his hoofs scudding up the soil.

He ran right under Humphrey's legs, and right past Emerald, who loved the smell of lavender so much that she followed him. Joshua and the bony danced round the field together and when the bony was too full of happiness to stand up he rolled over in the mud and kicked his legs in the air.

'We'll have to clean him before he has his dinner,' said Alison. 'I'll show you how to do it, Willa, and then it will be your job.'

'See how fat he is,' said Old Miss Annie. 'You can't call him the bony now, can you?'

'But I don't know what to call him,' said Willa. 'I can only think of Bony.'

The Shetland pony trotted up to them.

'He's getting as round and fat and bonny as a bee,' said Old Miss Annie. 'How about Bonny, Willa? It's a bit like Bony, but there's a world of difference between them, isn't there?'

And there is.

Vicky Fox

Deep in the earth it was brown and cool and it smelled of mushrooms and leaves. In the spinney woods a fox watched for the moonlight and streaked out from his lair. He put his snout to the ground to sniff out the trails he had made his own. He crossed the scents of rabbits and badgers and all the other creatures of the night. He smelled cats and dogs and human beings. He smelled the eggman's hens in the field at the edge of town.

In his lair his vixen lay with her brush tucked under her chin. She watched for the fox to bring her food. Her brown cubs nuzzled each other, snug at her side, and warm with her milk.

In the houses children were sleeping. In the house in the field at the edge of town a little girl called Ruth opened her eyes and listened. She could hear the hens screeching in the yard. She heard her father the eggman getting out of his bed, and she heard the stairs creaking. 'I'll get that fox!' she heard him say. 'This time I'll get him, good and proper.'

Ruth heard him going out to the yard. She could hear him untying the dogs.

'You shouldn't, you shouldn't,' the little girl cried. 'Killing the lovely foxes is cruel.'

And that was the night that the fox died. The dogs ran out to meet him, and he never went home again. The dogs ran on to the vixen's lair and found the vixen with her brush tucked under her chin. They found the nuzzling cubs that were warm with her milk by her side. And when the eggman whistled them home they left them all for dead.

But one of the cubs was still alive. She whimpered for her mother to give her milk. She whimpered for her brothers and sisters to nuzzle her. She whimpered for her father to come home. But nobody answered her.

The moon went dark, and all night long it rained. The rain hissed like long snakes, and all the leaves pattered and gleamed.

The fox cub curled up with her brush tucked under her chin and waited for food.

Fox in a box

Next morning the eggman went across the field to see what his dogs had done.

Well, he thought, *these foxes won't be after my hens again, that's for sure.* He was just about to go when one of the fox cubs opened her eyes, and the eggman saw that she was still alive. She was no bigger than a kitten, and she was as brown as a nut. She panted up at him with fright. He remembered what his daughter Ruth had said in the night. 'You shouldn't, you shouldn't,' she had cried. 'Killing the lovely foxes is wrong.'

The eggman picked up the fox cub by the scruff of her neck and tucked her under his arm so she wouldn't bite him. He took her into the house and put her down on the table.

'If you think killing foxes is wrong,' he said to Ruth, 'then make this one live.'

Ruth had no idea what to do with a fox. She put her in a box and fed her on milk and food scraps. She called her Vicky Fox. She daren't touch her, because her mouth was always open and her little rows of teeth were sharp and fine. She daren't stroke her or pick her up. But she thought the fox cub was so beautiful that she couldn't take her eyes off her. She just couldn't stop looking at her. She watched her for hours, and Vicky Fox curled up in her box and never took her eyes off Ruth.

Sometimes when Ruth went out of the room the cub would sneak out of the box and run across the carpet, run up and down the furniture, run under the table. But as soon as the door opened she would sneak back into her box and lie there, panting with fear, waiting for food, and watching.

She grew bigger and stronger, and her coat that was as brown as a nut turned a deep and rusty red, like oak leaves in autumn. Her eyes were like amber beads. She was beautiful. But Ruth daren't touch Vicky Fox in case she snapped her hand off, and she hated her smell.

'Put her out,' the eggman said. 'The dogs won't get her now. They're too used to her. And she won't get the hens. She doesn't know how to hunt. Let her go.'

'But I like having a fox for a pet,' said Ruth.

Vicky Fox curled up and watched her, panting with fear.

'What good is a pet that you're scared of, and that makes the house smell like a farmyard?' the eggman said. 'Wild things don't make pets. Let her go.'

'Will she die, if I let her go?' Ruth asked, and her father laughed.

'Of course she will,' he said.

Wily Ruth

But Ruth was wily. She put Vicky Fox out, but she didn't let her go. She put her box in a shed that her father never used. Cobwebs hung from the beams like old men's beards. Vicky Fox crawled under a wheelbarrow and peered out at Ruth. Her eyes were as bright as yellow lamps. Her tiny teeth gleamed. She panted with fright. Ruth closed the bottom door of the shed and watched her. She threw in some chicken scraps and Vicky Fox pushed them with her snout till they were hidden under a pile of straw.

'You're no good for a pet, you aren't,' Ruth told her through the top door of the shed. 'But remember who your friend is, Vicky Fox. You'd have died if I hadn't fed you and given you a home.'

Vicky Fox slunk into the shadows under the old wheelbarrow. She lay there, panting.

'Nobody else loves you, Vicky Fox, remember that,' Ruth said. She ran back through the yard, where the brown and red

hens clucked round her feet and bobbed about for grain.

When the yard was quiet Vicky Fox crept from her box. She lay still. It grew dark outside. Rain came down, and she could hear it, hissing like snakes. She listened for her mother to give her milk, and for her brothers and sisters to nuzzle her, and for her father to come loping home, but nobody came.

The visitors

Then one day somebody tried to help Vicky Fox, but she did it all wrong. This is what happened.

It was a day that was full of the end of summer. You know what it's like, when the sky is blue but there's mist in the air. When the leaves are turning to gold on the trees.

When the cobwebs are hanging with dew all day. That was the day the visitors came and one of them tried to help Vicky Fox, and she got it all wrong.

Ruth was sitting in her yard with the hens. She heard voices out in the lane, and she went to the gate to see who it was. She could see an old lady with hair like wool holding a little girl by the hand. The old lady had a stick, and the girl had a box. They were picking blackberries from the hedge, and the old lady was talking. But she had such a tiny whispery voice that it was hard to hear what she said.

'I used to bring Joshua along here for his walk,' the old lady was saying.

'Do you miss Joshua?' the little girl said.

'Oh, I do, Willa,' the old lady said. 'But he's happy in his field of goats.'

'And he's got Bonny to play with, Miss Annie,' Willa reminded her.

'Oh, yes,' Old Miss Annie said in her tiny voice. 'He's got Bonny to play with now. But I miss taking him for walks, all the same.' She saw Ruth watching them from the gate and she called out to her. 'Do you want to pick blackberries with us?'

Ruth ducked down to the hens so she couldn't be seen. She was a little bit scared of Old Miss Annie because she'd noticed how twiggy and twisted her hands were. But she liked her whispery voice. It made her think of morning mist on her field. She didn't like Willa because she held Old Miss Annie's hand as if she just didn't care how twisted it was. But she wanted to know who Bonny and Joshua were. So she said in a voice like a hen's, all clucky and high, 'There's plenty more blackberries in the field, you know,' and she ran and hid behind Vicky Fox's shed.

Old Miss Annie stopped by the gate. 'So there are,' she said. 'Beautiful blackberries, big and fat and bursting with juice, Willa.' Then she said in a voice loud enough for Ruth to hear, 'Doesn't the egg-girl's mother want them for jam?'

'She hasn't got a mother,' Ruth said in a voice like a hen. She liked the way Old Miss Annie said 'jam', making the word sound runny and sticky and sweet.

'Well, I'll make some for her and her father if she'll help me pick blackberries from her field,' Old Miss Annie said, and Ruth came out from behind the shed, a little bit shy, and opened the gate for them.

As they came into the field Old Miss Annie stopped and sniffed.

'Fox!' she said. 'I can smell fox around here.'

'She's my pet,' Ruth said. 'Vicky Fox.'

'Where is she then?' asked Willa, who didn't believe for a minute that Ruth could have a fox, even if she was the eggman's daughter and lived in a house in a field.

Ruth opened the top door of the shed and Willa stood on her tiptoes and they all peered into its darkness.

Run, Vicky Fox!

As soon as Vicky Fox heard the voices of strangers she jumped up on the beam of her shed. She ran backwards and forwards along it, backwards and forwards in the shadows among the cobwebs that hung like old men's beards. Her snout was down and sniffing her tracks. Her amber eyes gleamed as she watched Willa and Old Miss Annie and Ruth. Her mouth was wide open and ready to snap. She was panting with fear.

'She's beautiful,' Old Miss Annie said. Ruth nudged closer to her, and Willa had to move sideways. She didn't like Ruth one bit.

'And does Vicky Fox live here all the time?' Old Miss Annie asked.

'Yes,' said Ruth. 'She's my pet.'

'Oh, dear,' said Old Miss Annie.

'Can I stroke her?' asked Willa.

'You'd better not try,' said Ruth. 'Or she'll have you for her tea.'

Miss Annie sighed. 'I wish Vicky Fox could have a run,' she said in a tiny faraway voice that seemed to be thinking of woodlands.

And that was when Willa decided to help Vicky Fox, but she got it all wrong.

Old Miss Annie and Ruth started to pick the blackberries on the hedges. Willa trailed behind. She didn't like Ruth because Miss

Annie had given her the blackberry box to hold, and that was Willa's job. But Miss Annie's heart wasn't in blackberry picking.

'Look at the tracks in the grass that the animals have made,' she said. 'Badgers and rabbits and probably foxes, too. Poor Vicky Fox, stuck in a shed when there's all this grass and fox scent in the air! What a shame!'

'She'd have died if I hadn't fed her!' said Ruth, and when Miss Annie looked down and saw Ruth getting ready to cry she held out her hand. Even though it was twisted and knobbled like sticks, Ruth held it and found how soft and warm it was.

Willa snatched up the box and ran to the other side of the field and stuffed it with blackberries till it was ready to spill.

Before they left the field Old Miss Annie went to Ruth's house. She wanted to thank the eggman for letting her come into the field, though he was busy counting his money in the kitchen and didn't even know she had been.

'I'll make you some jam!' Old Miss Annie called through the door. 'And you and Ruth can have it for your tea.'

And it was while Miss Annie was talking at the door that Willa did what she did. She thought she was helping Vicky Fox, but she got it all wrong. She did it to please Old Miss Annie. And she did it because she didn't like Ruth, who was holding Miss Annie's hand.

It didn't take long to do. She opened the bottom door of the shed. And she said, 'Run, Vicky Fox. Run!'

Back to the spinney woods

At first nothing happened. The eggman was going to town and he gave them a lift to their road in his van, and on the way Old Miss Annie fell asleep, so Willa couldn't tell her then. When they arrived Miss Annie went straight to her house to make the jam and Willa had to go home for a bath, so she couldn't tell her then. She didn't tell anyone because she wanted Miss Annie to be the first in the world to know that she had given Vicky Fox a run. When she went to bed she dreamed of her streaking like wildfire through the dark woods, running with the other foxes through the night.

But it didn't happen like that. Long after Willa had gone, Vicky Fox stepped out of her shed. She took her time. She sniffed every bin in the yard. She sniffed at the cat, who just rolled away from her and wasn't afraid. She sniffed at the hens, who pecked and bobbed around her paws for grain. Then, sniffing every blade of grass, she started to cross the field. She crouched so low you would think she was melting into the earth. And through the bushes she went, through the blackberry brambles, and into the spinney woods.

During the night it rained. It hissed down like snakes, and the grass gleamed with it. Vicky Fox crouched down into the roots of trees, afraid. She remembered her mother's milk, and whimpered for it. She whimpered for her brothers and sisters to nuzzle her. She whimpered for her father to come home. She remembered the barking and snarling dogs and she panted with fear. The night moved with fear. Mice scampered across the grass. Rabbits thudded into their burrows. Vicky Fox watched and listened and smelled the animal air. She waited for someone to come and bring her food, but nobody came.

And in her room in the house in the field Ruth lay awake and cried. Her fox had gone.

Willa tells Old Miss Annie

Willa had to go to school next day. At tea-time Old Miss Annie came round with a jar of blackberry jam for her.

'This is the best jam I've ever made!' she said. 'And every time I eat it, I'm going to think of Ruth the egg-girl and Vicky Fox.'

That was when Willa remembered what she had done. 'Miss Annie!' she said, her voice sticky with bread and jam. 'Guess what I did!'

She knew how pleased Miss Annie would be. She licked all her fingers one by one. And then, because Old Miss Annie still hadn't guessed, she said, 'I gave Vicky Fox a run!'

She waited for Old Miss Annie to say how pleased she was.

But she didn't. She went quiet and sad.

'Aren't you pleased, Miss Annie?'

'No, Willa, I'm not.'

Old Miss Annie held Willa's hands and told her that Vicky Fox might die. 'She can't hunt for food. She's never been taught. She's a house fox, Willa. She'll never be able to live in the wild.'

'But you said . . . Oh, Miss Annie, you said that you wished Vicky Fox could have a run!' Willa could hardly speak, she was so afraid for Vicky Fox.

Old Miss Annie shook her head. 'Not that sort of run, Willa. Not a running-free run. I meant the sort of run that pet rabbits have. She'd have to have fences six feet high so she couldn't jump over them. And six feet deep so she couldn't dig under them. That's the sort of run that I meant, Willa.'

Willa closed her eyes and cried.

Come home, Vicky Fox

Old Miss Annie and Willa hurried down to the eggman's house. It was quite a long way, but they both ran for part of it. By the time they arrived they were puffing and out of breath. There was the house in the field, and there was the shed with the bottom door open, and there was Ruth, sitting outside it, waiting for Vicky Fox to come home.

They all went round and round the field calling out Vicky Fox's name. They looked under all the bushes and in all the caves the tree roots made and wherever the grass was high enough to hide a fox.

Then Willa crawled under a bramble bush and into the spinney woods and there she found her.

The fox was curled right round with her brush tucked under her chin. Her mouth was open wide and her little sharp teeth were gleaming white. Her eyes were like amber. She was panting with fright.

'I've found her! I've found her!' Willa shouted. 'I've found Vicky Fox!'

Old Miss Annie and Ruth crawled after her. Vicky Fox shrank back into the dark roots.

'She's frightened,' said Old Miss Annie. 'She's hungry and frightened, and she might bite. But leave her to me, Ruth, and I'll get her home safe.'

Ruth and Willa crawled back out of the brambles and sat looking at the see-through moon that was coming into the sky even though the sun was still shining.

'You go to my school,' said Ruth.

'Do I?' said Willa.

'I saw you this morning,' said Ruth. 'But I didn't play with you because I've been crying all night.'

'I don't play with anyone,' said Willa.

'Neither do I,' said Ruth. 'Nobody plays with me because I'm an egg-girl. They say I smell of hens.'

'You do a bit,' agreed Willa. 'Nobody plays with me because I talk funny.'

'You do a bit,' agreed Ruth.

They both stared ahead. The moon was bigger now. Nearly white.

'Anyway,' said Willa. 'Miss Annie's my friend.'

'Vicky Fox is mine,' said Ruth.

They could hear Old Miss Annie talking to Vicky Fox as if she were a baby, soft and quiet in her tiny, whispery voice. After a long time of just sitting quietly she knelt forward and reached out her hand to Vicky Fox. She picked her up by the scruff of her neck. She tucked her into her arms and held her jaw so she wouldn't bite. And she carried her over the field to her box in the shed.

Happy ending

You might think that is the end of the story, but it isn't quite. Next day Willa and Old Miss Annie went to the house in the field again. They had a jar of blackberry jam for the eggman, and he was so pleased that he gave them a box of eggs. Miss Annie had something else in her bag. It was a dog collar and a very long clothesline.

'What are you going to do with that?' Ruth asked her.

'I'm going to give Vicky Fox a run,' said Miss Annie.

It took her a long time to fasten the collar round Vicky Fox's neck, a lot of whisperings and shushings in her tiny voice.

Then she fastened the clothesline to the collar and told Willa to open the bottom door of the shed.

And out into the field they went. Vicky Fox darted from scent to scent. She could smell mice and badgers and rabbits. She could smell her own tracks. She crouched into the long grasses, and into the caves that the tree roots made, and under the brambly bushes. She rolled and ran, and always she kept her eyes on Miss Annie. Willa and Ruth had a go, tying the rope to their wrist, and they shrieked with laughter as Vicky Fox pulled them from one side of the field to the other.

At last, when they'd all had enough, they led Vicky Fox back to the shed and untied her rope. She dived into the straw in her box, safe and warm. And almost at once she fell asleep, snoring.

Now every day Old Miss Annie comes

to the field, when she isn't going to see Joshua, that is. She takes Vicky Fox for a run. It looks more as if Vicky Fox is taking Old Miss Annie for a run, the way she pulls her from one side of the field to the other, to the long grass and the roots of the trees and the brambly bushes where all the smells are rich.

Sometimes Willa comes with her, when she isn't going to see Bonny, that is. And when she does she runs in the field behind Old Miss Annie and Vicky Fox − playing with Ruth, her best friend.

About the Author

Berlie Doherty has twice won the Carnegie medal – for *Granny Was a Buffer Girl* and *Dear Nobody* – and was Highly Commended for *Willa and Old Miss Annie*. Her other titles include *Spellhorn*, *Children of Winter*, *The Snake-Stone*, and *Daughter of the Sea* (Writers' Guild Award). She has also written a volume of poetry, *Walking on Air*, as well as a number of television plays.

Also by Berlie Doherty and published by Catnip

Peak Dale Farm Stories

Valentine's Day

Berlie Doherty

Illustrated by Kim Lewis